D0501262

The LAST FIREHAWK

The Whispering Oak

by
Katrina Charman
illustrated by
Jeremy Norton

SCHOLASTIC INC.

The LAST FIREHAWK

Read All the Books

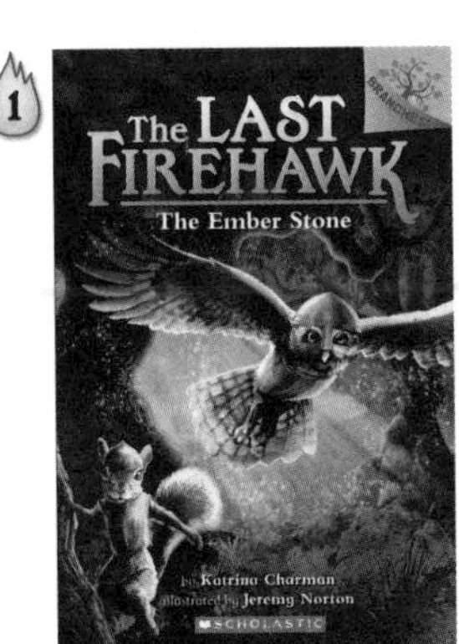

scholastic.com/lastfirehawk

Table of Contents

For Maddie, Piper, and Riley. —KC
Thank you to my parents, who showed me the value of art. —JN

Library of Congress Cataloging-in-Publication Data

Names: Charman, Katrina, author. | Norton, Jeremy, illustrator.
Title: The whispering oak / by Katrina Charman ; illustrated by Jeremy Norton.
Description: First edition. | New York, NY : Branches/Scholastic Inc., 2018.| Series: The last firehawk ; 3 | Summary: Tag the owl, Skyla the squirrel, and Blaze the young firehawk continue their hazardous journey to find and reunite the pieces of the Ember Stone, the only power which can defeat the evil vulture Thorn, and save Perodia.
Identifiers: LCCN 2017015813 | ISBN 9781338122558 (pbk.) |
ISBN 9781338122572 (hardcover)
Subjects: LCSH: Owls—Juvenile fiction. | Squirrels—Juvenile fiction. | Animals, Mythical—Juvenile fiction. | Magic—Juvenile fiction. | Quests (Expeditions)—Juvenile fiction. | Adventure stories. | CYAC: Owls—Fiction. | Squirrels—Fiction. | Animals, Mythical—Fiction. | Magic—Fiction. | Adventure and adventurers—Fiction. | Fantasy. | GSAFD: Adventure fiction. | LCGFT: Action and adventure fiction.
Classification: LCC PZ7.1.C495 Wh 2018 | DDC [Fic]—dc23
LC record available at https://lccn.loc.gov/2017015813

10 9 8 7 6 5 4 3 2 1 18 19 20 21 22

Printed in China 38
First edition, April 2018
Edited by Katie Carella
Book design by Maria Mercado

INTRODUCTION

In the enchanted land of Perodia, lies Valor Wood—a forest filled with magic and light. There, a wise owl named Grey leads the Owls of Valor. These brave warriors protect the creatures of the wood. But a darkness is spreading across Perodia, and the forest's magic and light are fading away . . .

A powerful old vulture called Thorn controls The Shadow—a dark magic. Whenever The Shadow appears, Thorn and his army of orange-eyed spies are nearby. Thorn will not stop until Perodia is destroyed.

Tag, a small barn owl, and his friends Skyla and Blaze, the last firehawk, have found two pieces of the magical Ember Stone. This stone may be strong enough to stop Thorn once and for all. But there are more pieces to be found. Thorn and his spies are also searching for the stone—and for Blaze. The friends' journey continues . . .

PERODIA
Shifting Sands
Whispering Oak
Mossy Hills
Howling Caves
Valor Wood
Rocky Beach
N
W
E
S

Crystal Caverns
Jagged Mountains
Bubbling Bog
Lullaby Lake
The Shadowlands
Blue Bay
Fire Island

CHAPTER 1

THE SHIFTING SANDS

Tag pulled the magical map from his sack. He looked at a glowing spot on the paper.

"We need to head west," Tag told his friends Skyla and Blaze. "The next piece of the Ember Stone should be at a place called the Whispering Oak."

Blaze peeped.

"We have to move fast to stay ahead of Thorn and his Shadow," Skyla said, looking to the sky for The Shadow's dark cloud. The sun was slowly rising above the trees.

Blaze leaned over Skyla's shoulder to look at the map. "Shifting Sands!" she said.

"We have to cross that?" Skyla asked, pointing to a large sandy desert.

Tag nodded. "Grey once told me that the Shifting Sands are full of swirling sand tornadoes."

Skyla shivered. "We're going to have to be *really* careful," she warned as Tag put the map away.

The three friends set off. Tag and Blaze flew overhead while Skyla raced through the trees below, zipping up and over branches in a blur of grey fur. The farther west they traveled, the warmer it became.

"Phew!" Skyla said as they rested by a small stream. "It's getting hot."

Tag's feathers ruffled in the warm breeze. "It's getting windy, too," he said.

Blaze pointed her wing ahead. "Shifting Sands," she said.

Tag flew above the trees and saw that Blaze was right. The trees thinned out and beyond that, as far as Tag could see, was the desert.

Blaze peeped at Skyla, turning so Skyla could climb onto her back.

"Great idea, Blaze," Skyla said as she climbed on.

"Yes," Tag agreed. "We can move *way* faster if we all fly."

They took off, soaring over the trees toward the sandy desert.

The closer they got to the desert, the stronger the wind blew.

Suddenly, Tag was blown out of the sky, onto the soft sand at the edge of the desert.

Blaze and Skyla landed beside him.

"The wind is too strong!" Tag yelled, spitting sand from his beak. "We'll have to walk through the sandstorm!"

The wind whirled around them, sending sand flying into their eyes and beaks. Tag used the dagger that Grey had given him to cut three strips from the top of his sack. He tied one over his beak to keep the sand out. He handed the other two to his friends, who did the same.

Tag dragged his feet across the desert, pushing against the wind and sand. Skyla and Blaze followed.

The wind blew stronger still. The strips of cloth flew from their faces, and the sand shifted beneath Tag's feet.

All of a sudden, the sand began to move across the desert like waves. Up and down. Higher and higher.

Tag glanced up just in time to see a huge swirl of sand heading right for them.

TORNADO!

"Sand tornado!" Tag cried.

The swirling sand tornado was ripping a path across the desert as it moved closer.

Tag reached for Skyla's paw, but a giant sand wave rose up, knocking Tag over! He started sinking beneath the sand as the wave pulled him farther away.

"Skyla! Blaze!" Tag cried out. He tried to fly, but the wind was too strong.

From the ground, all Tag could see was sand.

Skyla jumped onto Blaze's back as a big gust of wind pushed them forward to land next to Tag! Tag grabbed hold of Blaze's tail, and Blaze pulled as hard as she could until Tag was free from the sand.

"Are you okay?!" Skyla shouted.

Tag nodded. "Thanks for rescuing me."

But Skyla did not answer. She stared at something behind him, her eyes wide.

Blaze gave a loud warning, "PEEP!"

The sand tornado moved closer and closer.

Skyla grabbed Tag's wing. "We have to find shelter!" she cried.

Tag shook his head. "There's no time!" he replied, looking at his friends. "Blaze, you are the only one strong enough to fly out of the storm! You'll have to go on without us!"

Blaze stamped her feet. "No!" she cried.

The sand tornado was almost upon them.

Suddenly, Blaze raised her bright wings. Her feathers flapped in the wind, but she didn't fly away. Instead, she wrapped her wings around Tag and Skyla, making a cocoon. Then she ducked her head inside, bending low and digging her long talons deep into the sand.

Tag could hear the roar of the tornado as it surrounded them. "The tornado is on top of us!" he said, his feathers shaking.

Skyla's tail flicked back and forth. "I'm scared!" she yelled.

Tag reached for Skyla's paw, and Blaze gave a little peep.

The three friends clung to each other as tightly as they could, waiting for the tornado to blow them away.

A MAGICAL MEADOW

Slowly, the loud roar of the wind faded and the sand beneath their feet was still again.

"Has the tornado passed?" Tag asked.

Blaze lifted her head to look out across the desert. "Safe!" she said, opening her wings.

Tag blinked. He couldn't believe his eyes. The sky was clear and there was no sign that there had ever been a tornado.

"Look!" Skyla gasped, pointing to a deep groove in the sand. The tornado had passed right over where they stood.

Tag hooted in amazement. "I can't believe how strong your wings are, Blaze!"

Blaze smiled.

"You saved us!" Skyla told her, giving her a hug.

"Super-strong wings must be another of your magical firehawk powers," Tag said to Blaze. "Just like your firepower and your cry."

Skyla brushed sand out of her fur. "That was close. Even with Blaze's powers!" she said.

Tag checked that their piece of the Ember Stone was safe. Ahead, he could see a wide green line on the horizon. He pointed to it. "Do you see that?"

"We're near the end of the desert!" Skyla cried.

She raced across the sand. Tag and Blaze spread their wings and flew after her. As Tag neared the edge of the Shifting Sands, he could see the tops of lush green trees.

I hope there's water close by, Tag thought. He was thirsty after swallowing all that sand.

Tag and Blaze soon landed in a meadow of fruit trees. Skyla stood near a pool filled by a small waterfall. All around them were hundreds of colorful flowers. Tag took a deep breath. The air smelled so fresh.

“Where are we?” Skyla asked, picking a sparkly purple flower and tucking it beneath her armor.

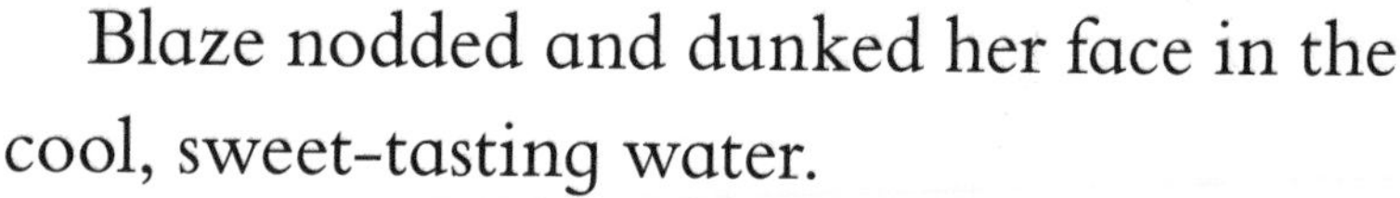

Tag looked at Grey's map, but there was no meadow. "I'm not sure. Maybe this is a magical place?"

"It sure feels like it," Skyla said.

Blaze nodded and dunked her face in the cool, sweet-tasting water.

The friends ate pineapple and mango and papaya until their tummies were full. Then they filled their water pouches and gathered fruit for the journey ahead.

Tag flew into the branches of a nearby tree. In the distance were two tall brown hills.

"We're almost at the Whispering Oak," Tag called. "We should keep moving."

"Can't we stay just a little longer?" Skyla begged.

"Peeeeep?" Blaze agreed.

"Thorn or his spies might be close behind," Tag replied. "We must go now."

The friends walked to the edge of the meadow. The dark shadow of the hills crept closer, and Tag shivered as the air grew cold.

Finally, they reached the foot of the two hills.

"The Whispering Oak is on the other side of these hills," Tag said.

TUNNEL OF SPIES

"We don't have to climb over these hills, do we?" Skyla asked, looking up at the two huge, craggy hills.

"Fly?" Blaze asked.

"There is a path through the middle of the hills," Tag said, pointing to a narrow tunnel. "That way will be quicker."

The three friends entered the tunnel between the hills. It was dark and cold. The tunnel was as wide as it was tall, and Blaze's head brushed the ceiling.

Everything was dusty and brown. A few bushes and trees grew out of the rock-covered hillsides, but they were all dead or dying.

"It looks like The Shadow has already been here," Skyla whispered, loading her slingshot.

Skyla might be right, Tag thought, pulling out his dagger. *I just hope Thorn hasn't already found the next piece of the Ember Stone.*

Skyla reached for her slingshot. "Do we have any more acorns?" she asked Tag. "I'm running low."

Tag felt inside his sack, then shook his head. "I'm sure there will be more at the Whispering Oak," he told her.

"Is our piece of the stone warm yet?" Skyla asked.

Tag checked their Ember Stone. The two pieces they had already found had joined together to make one stone. "It still feels cool," he said.

"Keep checking it. The stone will get warmer when we're close to the next piece," Skyla replied.

As Tag walked along, something **DRIP, DRIP, DRIPPED** onto his head. Tag shivered and wiped his face with his wing.

"It's too dark," Skyla said. "Blaze, can your wings light the way?"

Blaze gently flapped her wings up and down. One by one, her golden feathers lit up in flames to let out a soft glow. The light cast shadows along the walls and in the nooks and crannies in the grey rock.

Tag shuddered. *This tunnel is the perfect place for Thorn's spies to hide,* he thought.

Tag took the lead while Blaze followed, with Skyla keeping a lookout to the back.

"Stay on your guard," Tag whispered.

The tunnel grew narrower.

There was a cracking sound ahead. Sand and rocks fell away from the wall. Tag held his dagger tighter in his wing as creeping black shapes scuttled across the ground.

"We're not alone," Tag whispered.

CRAG BEETLES

"What was that?" Skyla squealed as something ran over her foot.

"Peep!" Blaze called. She shook her feathers until they got brighter.

Tag moved back against the tunnel wall and leaned down for a closer look.

Hundreds of shiny black beetles crawled out of gaps in the walls and ground.

"Crag beetles," Tag whispered. "They live inside cracks in rock and stone. Their shells are super-hard."

Skyla loaded her slingshot. "They might be Thorn's spies," she whispered. "Check their eyes."

Tag looked for the orange eyes that all of Thorn's spies had. But the beetles' eyes were hidden beneath their hooded shells.

"The beetles are small," Tag said. "Maybe they'll let us pass?"

SCRITCH! SCRATCH!

Blaze stamped her feet as a couple of beetles moved closer.

"The prickle ants were small, too," Skyla reminded her friends. "But they bit—hard!"

"We have to keep moving," Tag whispered. "Just try not to make any noise."

Tag tiptoed forward, slowly stepping over and around the crag beetles. He pointed his dagger at any that came too close. Tag could see a faint light at the end of the tunnel. "Almost there," he said.

Suddenly, one of the beetles dropped onto Tag's shoulder.

Tag jumped and his dagger fell to the ground with a loud **CLATTER!**

The beetles froze. They turned and looked up at Tag and his friends. A thousand glowing orange eyes stared up at them as they raised their razor-sharp horns.

"They *are* working for Thorn!" Tag gasped. He snatched up his dagger.

"Peep! Peep! Peep!" Blaze cried, her feathers shaking.

The crag beetles quickly flowed past the friends' feet like a thick, black river.

"What are they doing?" Skyla asked.

The beetles climbed on top of each other—one by one, until there were no longer hundreds of beetles but one gigantic, mega beetle!

How are we going to escape? Tag wondered. Blaze couldn't use her firepower—it would be too dangerous inside the small tunnel. So would her loud, piercing cry.

Tag raised his dagger. "We'll have to fight our way out of here!"

He charged with his dagger, knocking some beetles to the ground. Their shells were so hard that Tag couldn't hurt them. So he tried his best to break apart the mega beetle they had formed.

Skyla shot her last few acorns at the mega beetle. Beetles fell to the ground wherever she hit.

"I'm out of acorns!" Skyla called.

Tag continued using his dagger to break up the giant beetle, while Skyla attacked it with her paws and Blaze attacked it with her beak. Every time they knocked a few beetles away, more climbed into place.

"There are too many!" Tag shouted, backing away.

"Uh-oh," Skyla gulped.

SCRITCH! SCRATCH!

More beetles skittered behind the friends. Tag slowly turned around. Crag beetles had climbed on top of one another and formed a second mega beetle! Now there was one mega beetle ahead and one behind.

The friends were trapped!

TRAPPED!

Long shadows fell on the friends as the mega beetles moved closer. Blaze stamped her feet. The ground shook and Tag noticed a small hole near Blaze's feet.

"Look!" he said to Skyla.

Blaze stamped her feet, harder this time, and more of the ground fell away beneath her.

"Blaze is making a new tunnel," Tag said. "It's a way out!"

"Um, Tag," Skyla said, pointing.

The two mega beetles were closing in on them. Fast.

"Everyone, stamp your feet!" Tag ordered.

They stamped as hard as they could, making loud, echoing sounds inside the tunnel.

Suddenly, the ground gave way. The friends fell, down, down, down, sliding left and right, along the sides of the hidden tunnel.

"Wheeee!" Skyla called as they slid all the way through and out of the hill, landing with a thump on the soft grass outside.

Tag brushed the dirt from his feathers and looked back at the huge hole in the side of the hill. "We made it out!" he hooted.

A few crag beetles had followed them out of the tunnel. The beetles stepped into the daylight, hissing. Then they scurried back inside.

"The crag beetles don't like sunlight," Skyla said. "Just like Thorn's other spies, the tiger bats."

"They know we're here though," Tag said. "They will tell Thorn where we are. We have to find the Ember Stone before he sends The Shadow!"

"Oak!" Blaze peeped.

Tag and Skyla looked around. Everything was as dead on this side of the hill as it had been on the other side. A twisted, old oak tree stood in the center of a grey landscape. It was covered in odd-shaped green-and-brown leaves that Tag had never seen before.

Skyla pointed at Tag's sack. "Check the stone!" she said.

Tag looked inside, hoping to see a warm glow. But their piece of the Ember Stone was still cold.

"Maybe we're not close enough?" Skyla said.

The friends hurried down the hill to the Whispering Oak.

They searched in and around the tree for the stone. Blaze looked inside knots and on the lower branches. Skyla searched the base of the tree, collecting fallen acorns as she went, while Tag flew around the higher branches. But there was no sign of the Ember Stone.

I must be missing something, Tag thought. *But what?*

THE GRUMBLEBEES

"The next piece of the Ember Stone has to be here somewhere!" Tag said.

Blaze hopped around, searching beneath rocks at the base of the tree. Skyla climbed up to search among the higher branches. Tag flew overhead, searching the highest branches.

Suddenly, something caught Tag's attention. He could hear a low buzzing sound near his ear. He shook his head, but the sound continued. Tag swooped to the ground and hooted at his friends.

Skyla scrambled down the tree trunk.

Blaze hopped over, tilting her head to one side.

Tag held his wing to his ear. "Do you hear that?"

The friends listened carefully. Tag thought it might just be the breeze blowing the leaves, but the noise grew. It sounded like a whisper on the wind, becoming louder and louder.

Skyla's eyes widened. "Is the tree . . . talking?!" she asked.

The buzzing sound grew louder, until Tag could almost make out words. "Maybe it is . . . ," he said. "After all, it *is* called the Whispering Oak."

Tag jumped as a tiny voice shouted right by his ear: "Go away!"

The same thing must have happened to Skyla and Blaze, too, because they both jumped at the same time.

"Who's there?" Skyla cried, pulling back an acorn in her slingshot.

Tag felt something buzz past his face to land on a branch. He flew closer to see a small bee sitting on the branch. It was waving one of its legs at him. The branch moved and he saw another bee. Tag couldn't believe he hadn't noticed it before: The tree wasn't covered in leaves after all—it was covered in bees! But these were not normal bees. They were striped dark green and brown, and they had long, sharp stingers.

"What are you?" Tag asked.

"They might be Thorn's spies," Skyla whispered.

"We're not spies!" a small bee shouted. "We're grumblebees. Now get away from our tree!"

"But—" Skyla protested.

The grumblebees buzzed louder.

One by one, they flew from the branches until the oak tree was bare. They swirled in the air like a green-and-brown storm cloud.

"Peep!" Blaze called out to get the grumblebees' attention.

They only buzzed louder.

"Careful!" Skyla warned. "They might sting."

As the bees swarmed around Tag's head, he could hear hundreds of tiny voices shouting at the same time. They were all yelling over one another so the voices didn't make sense.

"I can't understand what you are saying!" Tag shouted at the grumblebees.

The grumblebees stopped shouting. They hovered in the air. Then, in a single voice so loud that it almost made Tag fall over, they shouted: "GO AWAY!"

THE BEARS

Tag, Skyla, and Blaze slowly backed away from the grumblebees. *Why are they so angry?* Tag wondered.

"What do we do now?" Skyla whispered, as the bees continued to surround them.

Tag tried to think of a way to ask the bees about the Ember Stone without making them angrier.

Blaze dipped her beak into Tag's sack and pulled out the Ember Stone. She held it high in the air so that the bees could see it.

The buzzing stopped.

Tag smiled at Blaze.

"We're searching for a stone that looks like this," Tag told the bees. "Have you seen it?"

One of the bees flew closer, examining the stone. Then it returned to the swarm. The bees buzzed and buzzed. Finally, the small bee flew back to hover in front of Tag.

"Where did you find that?" the grumblebee asked.

"Blaze found the first piece on Fire Island," Tag said. "She's the last firehawk."

The bees buzzed loudly when they heard this.

"We found the second piece in the Crystal Caverns," Skyla added. "And then our two pieces joined together."

"What do you want with the Ember Stone?" the grumblebee asked.

"We want to use it to stop Thorn and The Shadow from destroying Perodia," Tag said. "But we need all of the pieces of the Ember Stone so that it is powerful enough to defeat Thorn."

"We used to have a piece of it," the grumblebee told Tag. "But we don't anymore."

Tag looked around sadly. *If we don't find all the pieces*, he thought, *we'll never stop Thorn and we'll never save Perodia.*

"Our home was once a beautiful land filled with color and light," the bee said. "We were guarding the stone."

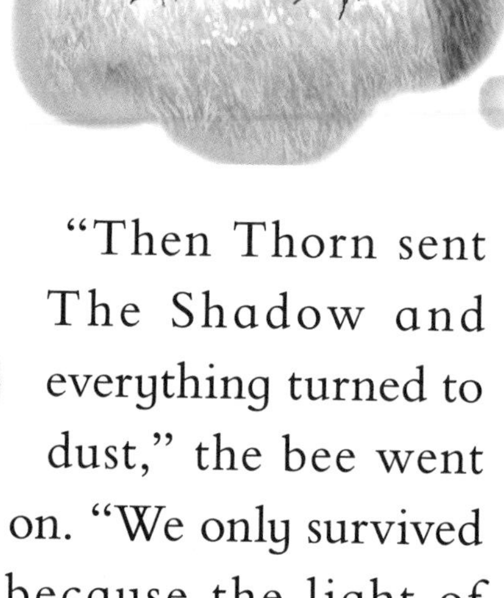

"Then Thorn sent The Shadow and everything turned to dust," the bee went on. "We only survived because the light of the Ember Stone scared The Shadow away."

Skyla gasped. "But if your stone scared Thorn away, when did he steal it?" she asked.

The grumblebees shook their heads. “He didn’t.”

Tag let out a sigh of relief. “So where is it now?” he asked.

The grumblebees started to buzz angrily again. “The bears stole it!” they said.

THE LAST HONEYCOMB

Tag frowned. "Bears?"

"Yes, the bears tricked us!" the small grumblebee said. "We had hidden our piece of the Ember Stone inside a honeycomb—in case Thorn came back for it. The bears said they would protect it, so we passed it to them for safekeeping."

"But they really just wanted to eat the honeycomb. They love honey!" added another grumblebee. "Now they won't give the stone back unless we give them more honeycomb."

The bees flew to the Whispering Oak, where a round beehive sat in the tallest branches.

"Thanks to Thorn, this hive is all we have left. It holds our very last honeycomb," the small grumblebee said. "We're sorry, but we cannot help you."

The bees disappeared inside their hive.

"We need to find the bears," Tag told his friends. "We have to make them give us the stone."

Skyla looked up at the beehive. "Where are the bears?" she called.

A small grumblebee flew out and pointed in the direction of the mossy hills that the friends had escaped from. The sun had already set and the moon was high in the sky.

"They live in a cave at the very top of that hill," the bee said.

Blaze yawned.

"We should rest here for the night," Tag said. "We'll talk to the bears in the morning."

"What about Thorn's spies?" Skyla asked.

"We will keep watch," the grumblebee said. "We'll warn you of any danger."

Then he went back into his hive, leaving the three friends alone in the darkness.

UNDER ATTACK!

The sun was rising as the three friends made their way up the hill. They walked beneath bare, twisted trees, over the dry grass.

Just then, Tag felt something hot against his wing. He opened his sack. The Ember Stone had started to glow purple! It was growing warmer and brighter by the second.

"Our piece of the stone is glowing!" Tag hooted. "We're getting closer."

Higher and higher they climbed, keeping an eye out for any of Thorn's spies, or worse—the dark cloud of The Shadow.

The air grew colder as they climbed, but inside Tag's sack, their piece of the Ember Stone grew hotter. When they were almost at the top of the hill, Tag heard loud snapping sounds in the air above. **CLACK, CLACK, CLACK.**

"Tiger bats!" Tag yelled, pulling out his dagger.

Skyla loaded her slingshot.

Tag looked up. Huge orange-and-black striped tiger bats soared overhead. Thorn's spies' orange eyes shone in the early morning sky, and their long, sharp beaks snapped at the air. **CLACK, CLACK, CLACK.**

"Peep!" Blaze cried.

The friends ducked behind a large rock, waiting for the tiger bats to attack. But the tiger bats didn't seem interested in them. They were circling above. Something had caught their attention farther up the hill: the bears' cave.

Tag gasped. "The tiger bats must know the bears have the next piece of the Ember Stone."

"Stone!" Blaze cried.

Before Tag could stop her, Blaze flew up the hill toward the cave.

"Blaze!" Skyla shouted, chasing after her.

Tag launched himself in the air, flapping as fast as he could to keep up. Up ahead, he saw the entrance to the bears' cave. A dull purple glow came from inside.

The Ember Stone! Tag thought. He could see their own piece of the stone glowing brightly inside the sack. It felt hotter than ever.

"We have to get that stone," Tag told Blaze and Skyla as he caught up with them. The friends hid behind another large rock beside the cave.

"How?" Skyla asked, pointing to the cave. The tiger bats were swarming the entrance. They were almost all inside, when—

GRRRRRRR!

A big, furry, brown blur charged out of the cave, chasing the tiger bats away. The bats flew into the air, then circled back to attack the bear. A second huge bear raced out of the cave, swiping his paws at the air. The tiger bats snapped at him with their beaks.

"We have to help the bears!" Tag said, gripping his dagger. He passed his sack to Blaze.

"Blaze, stay out of sight. Look after the map and our piece of the Ember Stone," Tag told her.

Blaze put on the sack and nodded.

Tag looked at Skyla. "Ready to fight?" he asked.

Skyla held up her slingshot and grinned. "Ready!"

She jumped out from behind the rock and aimed an acorn at one of the tiger bats. She hit it right on the head.

Tag followed, flying at the tiger bats with a loud screech. He waved his dagger, trying to draw them away from the cave so that Skyla might be able to sneak inside for the stone.

The tiger bats would not give up. They attacked again and again. Tag felt his wing getting weaker as he tried to hold off the bats.

The bears guarded the cave entrance, growling and swiping at any tiger bats who came near.

Skyla stood on top of the cave, shooting acorns at the bats below. But one of the tiger bats swooped up and knocked her over.

"Aghhhh!" she cried as she fell.

"Skyla!" Tag yelled. Tag tried to reach for her, but another tiger bat blocked his path. The bat knocked his dagger to the ground with its beak.

I can't hold them off any longer . . . , Tag thought, as the dark clouds of The Shadow began to form in the distance.

HERBERT AND HANK

SCREEECH!

Suddenly, Blaze ran out from behind the rock with her mouth open wide. Her wings glowed brighter than the Ember Stone. The tiger bats held their wings over their ears.

Thorn's spies quickly flew away—up into the darkening sky.

"Peep!" Blaze stared up at the sky, her feathers still burning brightly.

"Blaze, I told you to stay hidden," Tag said, crossing his wings over his chest.

Blaze's head drooped.

"But . . . I'm glad you helped us," Tag said, giving her a big grin.

"Are Thorn's spies gone?" a low voice boomed behind Tag.

Tag and his friends turned to look at the bears. "I think so," Skyla said, worn out from the fight.

"I'm Tag, and this is Blaze and Skyla," he said, pointing to his friends.

"Thank you for helping us," the bigger bear said. "I'm Herbert, and this is my brother, Hank."

Skyla's tail twitched. "The tiger bats will be back," she warned.

"They wanted our Ember Stone," Hank said. "But they can't have it!"

"Shadow!" Blaze peeped.

Everyone looked to the sky. Dark clouds had started to gather above two hills.

"Thorn will be on his way soon. The Shadow is already forming," Tag said. "We have to hurry."

Skyla turned to the bears. "We need your piece of the Ember Stone," she told them.

The bears growled. "It's ours!" Herbert said. "The grumblebees gave it to us! You can't have it."

Blaze pulled their glowing piece of the Ember Stone from the sack to show it to the bears.

"Blaze is the last firehawk. She is the only creature who can find all of the pieces," Tag said. "When the stone is complete, we can stop Thorn and The Shadow and we can save Perodia."

Hank and Herbert narrowed their eyes at the three friends. They whispered to each other in gruff voices.

Then they turned to face Tag.

"Why should we trust you?" Herbert asked.

Skyla huffed. "We just helped you fight the tiger bats!" she yelled.

"Peep!" Blaze nodded.

Herbert scratched his head. "Hmmm. That is true," he said.

He whispered into Hank's ear again.

"Okay," Herbert said, slowly. "We'll tell you the same thing we told those grumblebees: You can have the Ember Stone if you give us more honeycomb to eat. We finished eating the first one a long time ago."

Tag frowned. "We already spoke with the grumblebees. They only have one honeycomb left," he said. "They don't have any honey to spare."

"Well," said Herbert. "That is our offer."

Hank nodded and crossed his arms over his wide, hairy chest. "No honey. No stone," he agreed.

The bears returned to their cave.

CHAPTER 12

THE SHADOW MOVES CLOSER

The sky kept growing darker as the friends stood on top of the hill. They could see the Whispering Oak far away in the distance.

Tag sighed. He turned to his friends. "We must head back to the Whispering Oak," he said.

“Thorn could be here at any moment,” Skyla argued. “Why won’t the bears just give us the stone. We *did* help them fight the tiger bats!”

Tag looked around at the dry land. “Thorn destroyed this hillside. There is hardly any food left,” he replied. “I think Hank and Herbert really *need* the honey.”

“Well, then we’d better hurry,” Skyla said, climbing onto Blaze’s back.

The three friends glided over the hillside of dead trees. The sky was even darker when they arrived back at the Whispering Oak. The Shadow was moving closer.

"Bees!" Blaze called gently.

"Grumblebees!" Tag called, joining in with Blaze.

The tree's branches swayed gently as the grumblebees rose from them. The bees buzzed around the three friends.

"Did you find the next piece?" the smallest bee asked.

Tag nodded. "Yes, but the bears won't give it to us," he said.

The bees buzzed loudly.

"The bears have again asked for your honeycomb in exchange for the stone," Skyla told them.

The bees buzzed even louder.

"We only have one piece left and we need it!" the small bee told Tag. "When The Shadow destroyed our home, all the flowers were destroyed, too. We used to collect nectar from the flowers and put it inside our honeycomb. That's where we store our honey. But without those flowers, we cannot make any more honey. This piece of honeycomb holds the only food we have left."

The honey in that honeycomb is the only food left for the bees and for the bears, Tag thought. *What can we do?*

"Shadow!" Blaze called, pointing her beak to the sky. It was almost as black as night.

"Please!" Tag begged the bees. "Thorn and The Shadow will be here soon. Then all of Perodia will be destroyed. Even the Whispering Oak!"

Tag looked to Skyla for help, but she wasn't paying attention. She was digging around inside her armor.

"Skyla, what are you doing?" Tag said. "I need your help here!"

Skyla smiled as she pulled out the sparkly purple flower she had picked in the meadow.

The grumblebees hummed excitedly. They had caught the flower's sweet scent right away.

"What if I told you that there are still flowers close by?" Skyla asked the bees.

A NEW HOME

The grumblebees buzzed around the flower in Skyla's paw.

"Where did you find that?" they asked. "The Shadow destroyed everything. There *are* no more flowers."

Tag pulled out Grey's magical map. He unrolled it and pointed to the Whispering Oak. Then he slid his wing over the mossy hills and stopped at a spot on the other side. "This is where we found it—in a magical meadow."

"There are flowers of every color and soft green grass," Skyla said, smiling as she remembered.

Blaze nodded.

"You will be able to gather so much nectar and make so much honey that there will be enough for everyone—even the bears!" Tag added.

The smallest bee flew over and landed on Skyla's flower. He disappeared inside the petals and popped up a few moments later covered in pollen.

The other grumblebees gathered around, buzzing excitedly.

"What are you doing?" Tag asked. "Thorn will be here soon!"

The bees looked at Tag. "Follow us," the smallest bee said.

Tag flew up to the highest branch of the Whispering Oak, landing beside the large beehive.

"You may take what you need," the small bee offered.

"Thank you!" Tag said.

He peered inside and saw a golden honeycomb filled with sticky honey. Tag's mouth watered. It smelled delicious. *No wonder the bears want this so badly,* he thought.

He reached in with his wing and broke off the honeycomb.

Then Tag flew back down to Skyla and Blaze.

"Shadow!" Blaze peeped.

Tag could hear the grumblebees buzzing as they prepared to leave the Whispering Oak. *I hope they'll be happy in their new home in the meadow,* he thought.

The Shadow was almost overhead. The friends had to reach the bears before Thorn or the tiger bats did.

"To the hills!" Tag cried.

THE EMBER STONE

Tag, Blaze, and Skyla flew back up the hill as fast as they could.

"Fly faster!" Tag said.

They finally landed outside the bears' cave.

"We have your honeycomb!" Tag called.

Hank and Herbert peeked their heads out of the cave. "You do?" they asked.

Tag nodded. He reached into the sack where he had placed the honeycomb for safekeeping. Then he pulled it out to show the bears.

The bears licked their lips. "Yummy!" they said, holding their big paws out to grab it.

Tag held it back. "What about the Ember Stone?" he asked.

Skyla crossed her arms and nodded. "We had a deal," she said. "You'll get this honeycomb when you hand over the stone."

"Peep!" Blaze agreed, stamping her feet.

Herbert disappeared into the cave.

OWOWOWOOOOOOOOW! Herbert howled, then ran back out of the cave. He stood empty-handed, licking his paw. "I can't touch the stone!" he said between licks. "It's too hot!"

Blaze gave a loud peep.

"It's not too hot for Blaze," Tag said with a grin.

The bears stood back to let the firehawk pass into the cave.

Tag watched as the dark cave filled with purple light. Blaze hopped back out with the piece of the Ember Stone in her beak.

Tag handed the bears the honeycomb.

"Thank you!" Herbert said, chomping.

"Good luck with the rest of your journey," Hank said, licking sticky honey from his paws.

The bears headed back into their cave.

Blaze set the stone down on the ground. She took the other piece out of Tag's sack.

Both pieces glowed warm and bright. Slowly the pieces moved toward each other. The closer they moved, the warmer and hotter they became. With a bright flash of light, they joined to make one bigger piece!

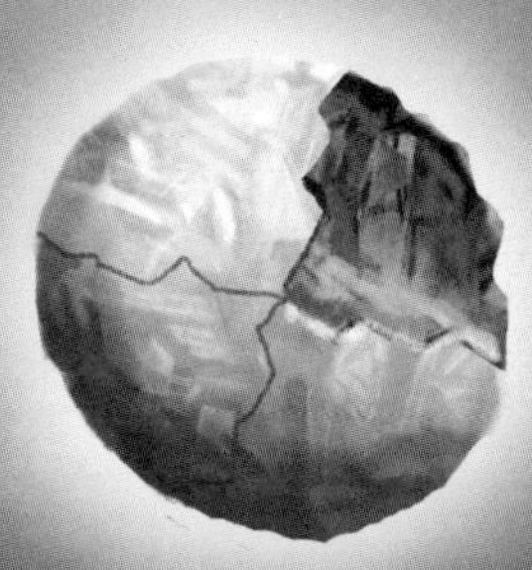

But the magical Ember Stone was still not complete. There was clearly at least one piece left for them to find.

Tag pulled out the map.

"Where to next?" Skyla asked as she peered over his shoulder.

Blaze hopped up and down excitedly as a new spot started to glow on the paper.

"East," Tag said, reading the map. "The next piece is at Lullaby Lake."

ABOUT THE AUTHOR

KATRINA CHARMAN has wanted to be a children's book writer ever since she was eleven, when her teacher asked her class to write an epilogue to Roald Dahl's *Matilda.* Katrina's teacher thought her writing was good enough to send to Roald Dahl himself! Sadly, she never got a reply, but this experience ignited her love of reading and writing. Katrina lives in England with her husband and three daughters.The Last Firehawk is her first early chapter book series in the US.

ABOUT THE ILLUSTRATOR

JEREMY NORTON is an accomplished illustrator and artist who uses digital media to develop images and ideas on screen with light. He was an imaginative and prolific artist as a child, and he still tries to convey that same sense of wonder in his work. Jeremy lives in Spain. The Last Firehawk is his first early chapter book series with Scholastic.

Questions and Activities

1. Why don't the crag beetles follow Tag, Skyla, and Blaze outside the tunnel?

2. The bears want honeycomb in exchange for the Ember Stone. Why do they want honeycomb? Reread page 76 for clues about what happened to their food.

3. The grumblebees leave the Whispering Oak to find more flowers. Why are flowers important to them?

4. Blaze's wings have lots of special powers. Find and retell two scenes where Blaze uses her wings to help her friends.

5. Tag, Skyla, and Blaze will need to journey to Lullaby Lake next. Draw a map of Lullaby Lake. What do you think this place will look like? What kinds of creatures will live there?